The Mermaid's Twin Sister

MORE STORIES FROM TRINIDAD

The Mermaid's Twin Sister

MORE STORIES FROM TRINIDAD

by Lynn Joseph

Illustrated by Donna Perrone

CLARION BOOKS

New York

The author would like to thank her aunts—Carmena, Sonia, Vilma, Zena—
and her mom, Janette, for their stories, their interest,
and their help in writing this book.

Clarion Books
a Houghton Mifflin Company imprint
215 Park Avenue South, New York, NY 10003
Text copyright © 1994 by Lynn Joseph
Illustrations copyright © 1994 by Donna Perrone

Illustrations executed in chalk pastel on colored paper.
Text is 12-point Sabon.
Design and typography by Carol Goldenberg.

Library of Congress Cataloging-in-Publication Data
Joseph, Lynn.
The mermaid's twin sister : more stories from Trinidad / by Lynn
Joseph ; illustrated by Donna Perrone.
p.   cm.
Contents: Keeping the duennes away—The mermaid's twin sister—
La Diablesse—Colin's island—Tantie's callaloo fete—The
obeah woman's birthday present.
ISBN 0-395-64365-1
1. Tales—Trinidad and Tobago. [1. Folklore—Trinidad and
Tobago.] I. Perrone, Donna, ill. II. Title.
PZ8.1.J76Me   1994
[398.2]—dc20   93-28436
                                    CIP
                                    AC

BP 10 9 8 7 6 5 4 3 2 1

*For my Aunt Joan, who generously
shared with me her stories of Trinidad
life, some of which I include in this
book. You are truly a special person in
my and Ed's and Jared's life.*

—L.J.

*To Michael, the light of my life.
The possibilities are endless.*

—D.P.

Contents

The Mermaid's Twin Sister

MORE STORIES FROM TRINIDAD

Note

My name is Amber, and my tantie tells the best stories in Trinidad. Trinidad is our Caribbean island. Tantie is my grandaunt. She helps to take care of all the little children in the family. In fact, she is the one who gathers all us cousins together to tell us stories at parties, at beach picnics, or just for so. Tantie's stories can be scary or funny, or tell us about our island a long, long time ago. What's most important about Tantie's stories, though, is that we don't forget them, because they are the real truth of Trinidad and of my family. Here are some of the stories I will always remember.

Keeping the Duennes Away

*E*VER SINCE TANTIE passed on her bamboo beads to me three years ago and told me I'd be the one to tell stories someday, everybody keeps waiting for me to tell a story.

But Tantie says not to rush. I have plenty of time to learn how to tell stories. And she says she still have plenty to tell, so all I have to do is watch and listen good. She says that's the best way to learn anything. And it's just what I did the day of our new cousin's baptismal.

My cousins Cedric and Susan had just gotten a new baby brother. Their parents, Uncle Thomas and Auntie Hazel, invited everyone to celebrate the baby's christening. Although Auntie Hazel is my daddy's sister, she invited family from my mama's side too—most importantly, Tantie. Tantie goes everywhere with us. She says her job is to keep track of all us cousins.

Anyway, everyone had arrived early at the church for the christening. Tantie was there looking sharp sharp in a big, flowered hat. Mama and Daddy wore their dark-blue church clothes and were speaking in quiet voices to Uncle Rupert and Auntie Ria, who sat in the same pew. They are Avril's parents.

Avril is the cousin I am closest to. He sat at the end of the pew next to me, his hair all slicked down neat neat. I was wearing a brand-new yellow dress Mama had made for the occasion. We didn't look like ourselves. Avril is thirteen years old, one year older than me. And he is bigger than me, and sometimes braver too. But we think alike. Tantie says we follow the same star. All I know is that Avril is my favorite cousin and my best friend. We closer than two breadfruits sharing a branch.

Our cousin Gerard came into the church with his mama, Auntie Mary, and his father, Uncle Willie, who's always smiling. Uncle Willie is my mama's brother. He carried huge bunches of buttercups and angel's trumpets and placed them near the altar. Everything was sparkling and ready for the big event.

Even the new baby was ready. He was dressed head to toe in shining white. Auntie Hazel held him carefully in her arms with Susan on one side of her and Cedric on the other. Susan's face had a mean scowl on it. She looked like she wasn't too happy with her new baby brother. Whenever he made a little cry, Susan inched farther away from him until she was almost on her father's lap.

Although the baby was a week old now, he still didn't have a name. Today was the day when he would get one.

We had been sitting in the church for a while, but we

weren't paying no mind to the time. Everyone was busy whispering to someone else, or praying, or just looking around. But then the new baby started to cry, and we began to notice that time was going by and there was no priest.

"This de right time?" Mama asked Auntie Hazel.

Auntie Hazel nodded.

"This de right church?" Uncle Rupert joked.

Everyone giggled. Then we got quiet and waited some more.

"I wonder what holding up this christening," Uncle Willie said out loud, louder than we talk in church.

Everyone began to look at the clock on the back wall. Some people stood up.

"I going to stretch my legs outside," Tantie said. "All yuh children want to come with me?"

Well, we jumped up fast fast to follow her out. But right then, a trembling Sister Ellen walked up to the front.

She wrung her hands and said, "Folks, I sorry to say we can't have de christening today. Father Bryon get lock up in his vestry by accident and we cahn get him out."

Well, that's when the confusion started. Auntie Hazel began to cry along with the new baby. Uncle Rupert started suggesting ways to get the priest out. "All yuh check for a window?" Tantie rounded up the smaller children and was herding them outside, so me and Avril followed. I could hear Tantie muttering something under her breath.

"Tantie, what you saying?" I asked.

Tantie shook her head. "I was only thinking that this de worst thing to happen. A christening cahn be stopped."

"Why, Tantie, we could just have it next week," I said. "Although all de food and drinks and party things fixed up and ready for this afternoon."

Tantie shook her head again. "This got nothing to do with de food and party. This got to do with de duennes."

And that's when I knew that Tantie go have to tell a story. Because Avril asked, "What are duennes, Tantie?" And to tell the truth, I wanted to know too.

Tantie made herself a seat under a lime tree on the side of the churchyard. We all settled down carefully in our best clothes. Then Tantie started her story.

"First of all, whenever a christening is planned, it must go on. That is de main thing. And it especially true for new children."

Tantie stopped talking and looked up at the sky. Then she began again.

"Once a long time ago, de priests used to go to wherever a new baby was being born, and they would baptize de baby right away so that if de baby died, its little spirit would go to heaven. Well, after a while, de priests stopped going around to de houses and de hospitals. There were too many babies being born and they couldn't be everywhere at de same time. So they decided to hold baptismals in church and anybody could come. De parents and godparents would plan a big party to celebrate the baby's baptismal.

"Sometimes, a child would not get baptized in time. Then de wood fairies would steal away de child's soul and make it a duenne. De duennes play and sing in de woods with de fairies, and they learn all kinds of tricks and get into plenty mischief.

"But medicine and hospitals got newer and better. Almost no babies die now. And de duennes are mad because they want more little babies to come and play with them."

"Tantie, what these duennes look like?" asked Cedric. He is twelve years old, like me. He tries to get right to the bottom of things.

Tantie looked out in the woods behind the church as if she saw a duenne. All of us turned around, but Tantie was talking again.

"They have feet that are turned backwards and they have no faces, except for small mouths, because they like to eat de sweet juicy fruit from de trees. They wear large, mushroom-shaped straw hats on their heads, and most of them have pigtails. Besides de fruit, they like to eat young corn and crabmeat.

"Anyway, de duennes began to come up with tricks to stop a baptismal so that de baby wouldn't be baptized. Then they would call to de nameless baby in sweet duenne voices that no one else could hear, hoping to get de baby's soul to come to de woods and play with them."

"Tantie, you think they go try to take our baby?" Susan asked in a hushed voice.

Tantie patted her head. "Only one way to stop de duennes when they start to sing to a new baby. You must hug de baby and sing to him too. Because then he won't hear de duennes' voices. He will only hear yours."

"Tantie, you think is those duennes that lock up Father Bryon in his vestry so he can't get out?" Cedric asked, standing up and putting his hands on his hips like he ready to fight.

"I wouldn't be surprised," said Tantie. "De duennes been up to their tricks for a long, long time. In fact, one time Uncle Willie himself stopped a prank by de duennes."

"My daddy?" asked Gerard.

"Yes, your father. He was about fourteen years old and was living down south in San Fernando."

"My mama was there too?" I asked, because Mama is Uncle Willie's sister.

"Yes, Amber, Sylvie was there—only 'bout ten years old. But she was de one who like to go and watch de baptizing down at Flat Rock."

"What's Flat Rock?" asked Gerard, leaning forward.

Tantie throw up her hands. "All yuh shush and I'll tell yuh de whole story." We all sat quietly, and she went on. "Well, every September, I would go down San Fernando to visit my sister Agnes and her children. Willie and Sylvie were de youngest ones, still living with their mother in de small wooden house halfway up a hill overlooking de sea. At de bottom of de hill by de sea was Flat Rock. It was a huge flat rock that de children would dive off into de sea when de tide in. When de tide out, de rock was black and shiny in de sunlight. We would all go down there with our cups of pepper sauce and pick oysters off de rock and break them open. Then we would dip de oysters in de pepper sauce and eat them. Was de best food in de world.

"Sometimes, early early before de sun even begin to think of coming up, de Baptists would hold a christening down at Flat Rock. We could hear them coming from a long way off. First we would hear their voices singing loud, sweet songs in de dark air. Then we would hear all their feet go swishing by in de road outside. And Sylvie would shake us and tell us to come on. 'Let's go see de christening,' she'd whisper.

"So we would get dressed and walk down to Flat Rock to watch."

"You went too, Tantie?" I interrupted.

"Yes, and it was somethin' to see, because de minister had a tall wooden staff and he had to wade far far out in de water with it. Then when he had gone far enough, he would stick it in de sand deep below de waves and make it stay there. And he would wade back in close to de shore, where he would baptize de person. De staff had to be standing up straight looking to heaven before de baptismal could go on.

"Well, one time after de minister had swum out and stuck de staff in de sand and waded back in, we all looked to be sure de staff was standing tall toward heaven, but it was gone.

" 'De staff floating away!' Sylvie cried.

"De folks on de shore looked sad. De young girl waiting in de sea for her baptismal looked sad. Some people even began to cry. But no one did anything because de staff was floating far away and almost out of sight.

" 'Look like no baptismal today, folks,' de minister said quietly.

"But just then we heard a splash. We turned around and

Willie was gone. His clothes was in a heap on Flat Rock, and when we looked in de water we could see his head bobbing up and down as he swam ahead in de dark sea.

" 'Willie, come back,' Sylvie called. 'Tantie, make him come back.'

"But all I could do was put my arm around her and pray. Everybody stood stock still and watched and waited. We couldn't see Willie anymore."

"What happened to my daddy?" asked Gerard in a scared voice. Tantie put her arm around Gerard the way she must have done with Sylvie. She looked at him as she told the rest of the story.

"After a long while, de sun suddenly broke through de sky, and slim pink rays came shooting up all over de edge of de sea. And there was Willie, swimming back in, pulling de staff behind him. When he was still a good ways out he stuck de staff deep down into de sand and tested it for firmness. Then he began swimming back toward Flat Rock."

"Daddy did all that?" Gerard asked. A big smile was on his face.

"Yes, Gerard," said Tantie. "And yuh should have seen de happiness he bring to all those people.

"Me and Sylvie cheered. De people on de shore clapped. De girl in de water cried happy tears. And de minister smiled.

"Willie swam up strong strong, not even out of breath. And de minister continued with de baptismal."

"So was de duennes that knock de staff over and make it float away?" I asked.

Tantie nodded. "Or so we thought, even though de girl

being christened that day wasn't no baby. Duennes usually de ones playing tricks at baptismals."

Susan stood up. "I going inside to sing to my new baby so de duennes won't get him," she said.

Tantie smiled at her and stood up too. "Let's all go inside and sing for de new baby."

And as we all began to walk inside the church, Mama came running out. "All yuh come on," she called. "It getting ready to start. Uncle Willie get de priest out de vestry. He figure out that lock somehow."

As Avril and Susan and them ran ahead, I turned to Tantie. "Uncle Willie must have some special power over de duennes. He keep outwitting them."

Tantie looked serious. "Your Uncle Willie just know that a christening cahn be stopped."

Later, as the priest sprinkled holy water on the baby's head, the godparents announced that the new baby's name was William. Uncle Willie couldn't stop smiling for the whole rest of the day.

The Mermaid's Twin Sister

EVERY SUNDAY, after Mama, Daddy, and me come back from church and eat lunch, we pack up the car and go to Maracas Beach. At the beach we find a good spot between two coconut trees and lay out the towels. Then Mama sits and reads a book and Daddy and me carry the rubber raft down to the water and pretend we are sailing for a new island.

But on one Sunday of the year we never ever go to the beach, and that is Easter Sunday. In fact, nobody I know goes to the beach on that Sunday. We go to church and then come home and eat a big lunch, but we don't do anything else for the rest of the day. All we do is sit on the porch and watch the sun set. Every Easter I asked Mama why we can't go to the beach like other Sundays. But she would only shake her head and say, "Because I say so."

Then this Easter she told me why. She said, "Amber, if you swim in de sea on Easter, you go turn into a mermaid and you go never come back."

I could see from her face that she wasn't joking.

When I asked Tantie about it later, she nodded her head. "Your mama didn't tell you before, cause she 'fraid you go want to try it and see for yourself. But is true, and those mermaids never come back from de sea."

"But Tantie, who all yuh know went swimming and turn into a mermaid?"

Tantie gave me a look that say, "You go doubt me?"

I glanced away. But I was feeling doubtful. I mean it wasn't like I ever hear Tantie or Mama say they saw a mermaid. And I sure never did see one. But I didn't say another word. And Tantie went on inside the house to talk to Mama, leaving me outside watching the sun go down and wondering what would really happen if I went swimming on Easter Sunday.

A few days later, Tantie came over and brought a friend with her. Her eyes were gray and quiet like the early morning mist that rise off the sea in the rainy season. And her skin was smooth and bright like polished stones. She had long, black hair that wrapped around her shoulders like a pair of arms.

"Amber," said Tantie, "this is my good friend, Miss Pascal. We known each other since we both younger than you."

I smiled at Miss Pascal and kissed her cheek. But I was wondering if I had heard right. This woman couldn't have grown up with Tantie. She was much younger. She looked even younger than my mama. But when she said hello, her voice was crackly like dried coconut tree branches.

Tantie and Miss Pascal stayed for the whole afternoon. Mama brought out a tray with tall glasses of mauby and a plate of currant rolls and guava jam and we sat on the porch, eating the sweet rolls and sipping the spicy coldness. Then the sun started going down and the crickets began singing. Tantie and Miss Pascal were talking about old times. Mama picked up some sewing from her basket. And I sat there watching as people passed by on the street.

Then I heard Miss Pascal say softly to Tantie, "I don't know how long Tilly go stay with them mermaids. Been over fifty years now."

Well, I didn't understand that at all. I kept real quiet and wished those crickets would hush up so I could hear.

"You know," Miss Pascal went on, "I always wonder what she doing with those mermaids all day long. Delphine, you think they having a good time down there?"

I could feel, more than see, Tantie shrug her shoulders. "I don' know, Jill. But Tilly always loved de sea more than all of us, so she bound to be happy there."

Well, I couldn't take it no more. I turned around so that Tantie could see I was listening to them. I was hoping she would tell me who Tilly and the mermaids were before I burst from not knowing. Tantie looked at me real seriously and said, "You want to know what happen?"

I nodded my head and sat down fast fast between their

chairs before she could change her mind. I waited for Tantie to tell the story, but it was Miss Pascal who started to speak.

"I was there," she said, "when my twin sister Tilly turn into a mermaid."

"What?" I shouted. "Your sister is a mermaid?"

Tantie put a hand on my shoulder. I sat back and tried to control the trembling that was taking over my body.

Miss Pascal started her story again. "Fifty years ago, me and my twin sister Tilly were twenty years old."

But I gasped out loud. Something terrible was happening here. Miss Pascal was a young woman! "Miss Pascal, you not seventy years old," I wailed.

Tantie patted my arm and kept her hand there. I got quiet.

"Me and Tilly were exactly alike," said Miss Pascal. "We looked de same. We walked de same, and we dressed de same. We even liked de same things. More than anything else, we loved de sea. Every day when we were little girls, we would go down to de sea and count shells or make rafts from fallen tree branches and seaweed ropes. When we got older, we would go to de sea after work and swim. We swam like fish far, far out in de sea."

Miss Pascal stopped and took a deep breath. Tantie handed her the glass of mauby. I was going to ask a question, but Tantie pressed on my arm, so I kept quiet. Then Miss Pascal went on.

"I think Tilly began liking de sea even more than me. She never wanted to do anything else but float over de waves or dive deep down and touch de bottom. I started liking other things besides de sea. And sometimes I just wanted to read a book instead of going to de sea. But Tilly went every day.

"Then one Easter Sunday, when no one goes swimming ever, Tilly decided she would go.

" 'Tilly,' I begged, 'don't go today. You know no one supposed to go swimming on Easter.'

"But she didn't listen to me. She went down to San Souci, which right next to where we lived in Toco, and she waded far, far out. I followed Tilly to San Souci and stood on a rock to watch her because I did not know what else to do. De tide was out and for a long way de water only came to Tilly's knees. Then she was so far out that I could barely see her. I watched her tiny body dancing with de waves. I was hoping she would have de sense to come back in quick before anyone would see she was swimming on Easter.

"But Tilly just kept on dancing with de waves, waving her arms in de air like a water fairy. I shaded my eyes from de sun and watched as hard as I could. But then I couldn't see her anymore. I took off my Sunday dress and waded in."

"Miss Pascal," I interrupted, "you went swimming on Easter Sunday too? And you not a mermaid!" I gave Tantie a look as if to say, "See?"

"Miss Pascal not finish, Amber," said Tantie.

Miss Pascal took another sip of mauby. I could see she was having a hard time telling this story, so I reached up and put my hand on her knee. "Is okay. You don't have to finish de story," I said. Although I was dying to find out what happen next.

Miss Pascal shook her head. "No, de rest of de story is de most important.

"I swam out to where Tilly had been. But she was gone. I dove beneath de waves and looked for her. I shouted her name. I swam up and down and all around for a long time until I was so tired, I didn't think I could ever swim back in. I turned on my back to float and rest and think what to do. And that's when I saw her.

" 'Tilly?' I called softly. 'Is that you, Tilly?' I was whispering because my voice was hoarse from shouting.

"But she didn't answer. She swam in front of me, pulling my long hair gently so I drifted behind her. She was heading toward de shore. And she swam quick like a fish, slicing through de water even smoother than she ever had before.

"And when we got to de shallows, she let go my hair and whispered in a voice that sounded like a cloud floating on de sea, 'Jill, I'm one of them now. But they think you're my spirit floating on de sea. They don't know it's two of us. So go now and be my earth self, and I'll be your water self.'

"Before I could answer, she turned fast and swam away. And all I could see was a long, beautiful fish slicing de waves."

Miss Pascal stopped talking and picked up her mauby glass again. I sat on the floor and not a word could come out my mouth. Tantie and Mama didn't say anything either.

Then far off in the clear evening air, I heard the happy notes of a steel band playing. We sat and listened until it stopped. The stars had come out bright bright in the dark sky, and Miss Pascal sat glowing in starlight.

"Tilly never came back," she said softly, looking right at me. "And I never grow old."

Daddy came home soon after that and drove Miss Pascal home. I stayed outside on the porch with Tantie, feeling the night's sweet coolness all around me.

"Amber," Tantie said in a soft voice, "Miss Pascal is de same way for de past fifty years. She look de same now as when she and Tilly went swimming on that Easter Sunday. And she say de only reason she didn't turn into a mermaid was because de sea was confused. It didn't know was two of them. So Miss Pascal got away. But she knows de truth of swimming on Easter Sunday, and she wanted to tell you herself."

"But how she could look de same after all these years, Tantie?" I asked.

Tantie shrugged. "I en know, chile, but it have something to do with her twin sister, Tilly."

"Maybe she want to stay de same so Tilly would recognize her if she came back from de sea," I suggested.

"Maybe," said Tantie. And both of us got quiet with our own thoughts.

I know I go never ask to go swimming on Easter Sunday again.

La Diablesse

ONE THING I NOTICE about storytelling is that you can find a story anywhere. At least Tantie seems to. One time she even told us a story from Trinidad's history, and it was one of her best ever. Me and Avril used to think history was so boring until we heard Tantie's story.

It was a pitch-dark night. Tantie had come over to my house to watch us cousins while our parents went out to a big fete. Rain was lashing the windows. Tantie came in wiping the raindrops off her forehead.

"Lightning dancing at de devil's tea table," she muttered.

We hurried to close all the windows, but the rain mist seeped in underneath the doors and through the latticework at the top of the walls. It was the kind of night where every noise sounds like jumbies rattling the windows, trying to get in from the rain. And every flash of light brightened the dark corners of the world outside so you could see the jumbies, if you brave enough to look.

After Tantie put the baby cousins to bed, she leaned back on the couch, put up her two feet, and closed her eyes. Neither Avril, Susan, Gerard, Cedric, or me felt like sleeping, but we figured we might as well get under the covers. All of us were afraid to sleep too close to the bedroom windows, for fear of the jumbies trying to claw their way in, so we piled close together on the rug of my bedroom.

After a while, the storm quieted down and everybody went to sleep. I was half asleep and happy to have my cousins close. But then I heard a noise. *Clang! Clang! Ting-a-clang!* It was moving near the windows. As I listened, it faded away a little but I could still hear it. *Clang! Clang! Ting-a-clang!*

The noise moved to the side windows, then kept going around the house. Then it came back again. But this time I heard something else. In between the *Clang! Clang! Ting-a-clang!*, I heard a dragging sound and a *Clop, clop,* as if the jumbies were tapping a hammer on the cement walkway. So it was *Drag, clop, clang! Drag! Clop! Ting-a-clang!* over and over, and the noises circled the house a second time.

Well, when I felt a hand touch my arm, I jumped and a scream caught in my mouth. But it was only Avril.

"Did you hear that?" he asked.

"Yes," I whispered. "What is it?"

I could feel him shrug. Then we heard Cedric and Gerard mumbling.

"Shh," I said. "Listen." So we all listened as the *Drag! Clop! Clang!* went past the windows again.

"What's that?" Susan cried.

"You asking me?" Cedric squeaked in fright.

Then a large darkness filled the doorway.

"Ahhh!" Susan screamed.

We dove under the covers and held tight to each other.

"All yuh children still awake?" asked Tantie.

We peeked out from the covers and watched as Tantie walked bold bold into the room and straight for the window.

"Tantie, you en hear that noise circling de house?" asked Avril.

Tantie pointed to the window. "You mean La Diablesse?" she asked.

"Who?" I whispered, because the noise was close to the windows again.

Tantie pressed her face to the windowpane. I clutched Avril, afraid the jumbies or whoever it was would snatch Tantie through the glass.

Tantie leaned back and shook her head. "It too dark for me to see outside, but I think is La Diablesse. She comes out at night, especially in storms."

The noise droned away and then suddenly got louder. *Drag! Clop! Clang! Clang!* The clang sounded a bit like a bell ringing.

After the noise faded again, I asked, "Tantie, who's La Diablesse?"

Tantie pulled the curtains firmly over the windows and walked over to our huddle.

"All yuh didn't learn about La Diablesse in history class?" she asked.

"No, Tantie," Susan and Cedric said together.

"I en remember no La Diablesse," Avril said firmly.

"What history class have to do with that noise outside?" I asked.

Tantie didn't answer right away. She left the room and us sitting half under our covers shivering and whispering about who La Diablesse could be.

"It sounding like one of Tantie's scary friends to me," Avril muttered. "Like de jumbie neighbors she got."

"No," I said. "Tantie's voice sounded kind of sad. Like she sorry for La Diablesse, not like it's a scary friend at all."

Then the noise came real close to the windows and we dove back under the covers and trembled together like a pile of guppies.

"All yuh can't let La Diablesse scare all yuh," said Tantie, coming into the room with a ray of light from a candle.

"Tantie," I squeaked, "La Diablesse will know we in here if she see de light."

Tantie put the candle holder on the floor and sat down. She rearranged her dress and tucked it all around her. Then she leaned back on my bookcase and sighed a big sigh.

"All yuh ready for some history lesson?"

Me and Avril looked at each other with disgust, but we didn't say anything because the *Clang! Clang!* was coming around again. This time it sounded like it was in the room with us. Although I wasn't too sure this was the time or place for a history lesson, we all huddled closer to Tantie and waited for her to begin.

"De first thing all yuh must know about La Diablesse is that they say she de cause of many deaths," Tantie said solemnly.

"Oh, no," I groaned softly.

Me, Avril, Cedric, Susan, and Gerard threw our arms around each other and held tight.

"De second thing all yuh must know is that La Diablesse not interested in children like you at all."

"That don't help us, Tantie," said Avril. "Cause she out there now." He pointed to the windows.

Tantie looked at Avril. "Well, maybe she realize we have a soon-to-be man right here. One who not a child anymore. Because that's who La Diablesse lures away—men!"

Although it wasn't funny, I almost laughed out loud when I saw the look that came across Avril's face.

"I not a man, Tantie," he said. "I still too young, too small, I just turn thirteen." I never heard Avril speak so fast.

Tantie didn't answer. She went on with the history lesson.

"A long, long time ago, when de Savannah was still a sugar plantation belonging to a fancy French settler, there were still a few Arawak Indians living on Trinidad. A lot of de Arawaks had been killed by fierce Carib Indians, and by settlers and their diseases, but some still lingered on. One of them was a beautiful Arawak girl named Suki. Suki had long, black hair that showed de stars and de moon in its shine. And she had sharp eyes that looked clear through people to their hearts inside."

"What did she see in their hearts, Tantie?" Susan whispered.

"Well, in some of them she saw happiness and in some of them she saw sadness and in some people she didn't see anything because their hearts were covered."

"Covered with what?" asked Avril. He was holding one hand over his heart as if to hide it.

Tantie looked at Avril. "Some hearts were covered with ice that even de hot Trinidad sun couldn't melt. And some hearts were covered with questions that nobody could answer. But Suki left these people alone. They did not understand her lovely island. They could not feel de island's blueness and greenness de way Suki could when she ran.

"Suki ran like a sea breeze. She skimmed over de shallow waves and flew through de jungle, never slowing down except to whisper hellos to de birds. All de new people coming to Trinidad on de big ships wondered how this beautiful Arawak girl's feet could fly.

"One day, a Frenchman in charge of de big ship saw Suki and ran after her. But he made heavy splashes in de pools of water and left big prints on de sand. And he couldn't catch Suki.

"De next day, he waited for her and tried again. This time he took off his boots and ran almost as fast as she did. But still, he couldn't catch up with Suki.

"After a few more days of running, de French captain ran right alongside Suki and smiled at her. She smiled back, then stopped all of a sudden.

"De Frenchman stopped too, but he pitched forward into a pile of seaweed. When he sat up, seaweed hung from his hair and over his ears and eyes. Suki pointed at the seaweed man and laughed. At first, de French captain turned bright red, but then he laughed too. And they became friends."

Tantie's story was going so good that nobody seemed to

be listening out for La Diablesse anymore. But I could still hear the *Clang! Clang!* and the *Clop! Clop!* outside.

Tantie took a deep breath and went on.

"Every day de French captain and Suki ran alongside each other, over de waves and through de jungle, as she collected fruit for her mother to eat and empty shells for making jewelry.

"One day, de French captain described a fete de new people were having and invited her to come.

"Suki's mother told her she should not go to the Frenchman's party. 'Arawaks are leaving this island tonight,' she told Suki. 'You must come with us.'

"But Suki did not want to leave her island or de Frenchman. So she watched sadly as her mother tied up their mats and some food and sailed away in search of another island where they would not have to worry about de new people's diseases."

"Suki stayed all by herself, Tantie?" I asked.

Tantie nodded yes. Then she put a finger to her lips to shush us. The *Clop! Clop!* and *Clang! Clang!* were going by again. We all huddled even closer together.

After the noise faded away, I whispered, "Tantie, how Suki could stay all by herself so—she not going to be sad?"

I could see a small smile on Tantie's face in the flickering light. It was a strange smile. Then Tantie said, "Amber, Suki made her choice from what she saw in de Frenchman's heart."

"What she see? What she see?" asked Susan.

"Love," said Tantie. "Now let me go on with de rest of

this story before that noise outside decide it go come in here."

"Ahhhh!" all of us squealed and pulled the covers tight up to our necks.

Tantie continued. "Suki went to de big fete in de Savannah. She looked at de bright cloth that hung from de ends of tall poles and fluttered in de breeze. She saw a pig and a goat roasting over two big fires. She watched as red-faced people danced in and out of big circles. They wore so much clothes that Suki thought that must be why they couldn't run.

"As Suki walked closer, men took off their black hats and waved them at her. She waved back, but she had no hat to bend low over. She did have beautiful shell necklaces and earrings and ropes of seashells tied around her wrists and ankles. In de firelight, her black eyes shone with a power so strong that all de men stopped talking and watched her. But her strong eyes looked right through them searching for only one man.

"Then she saw him. Her French captain walked over to Suki and took her hands in his. She was glad she had stayed behind.

" '*Je t'aime*,' he said, smiling.

" '*Je t'aime*,' she repeated.

"Then their hands fell back to their sides and only de light in their eyes touched.

"Suddenly, de moon slid behind a huge dark cloud. A deep rumble shook de ground. A blinding light streaked down from de sky, and with a fierce roar it struck Suki's beloved French captain to his death.

"Her scream was a silent one, but it flew over de earth and over de stars to de heavens. And although she did not make a sound, everyone covered their ears against de pain of her soundless scream.

"De next day, as they laid her beloved French captain in de earth, Suki cut off her right foot. She placed it in his grave so that they could run together over de clouds and through de heavens, always next to each other.

"De Frenchmen did not understand why she cut off her foot. They thought she was a devil woman. They named her La Diablesse. They shouted that she had lured their captain to his death. And after binding her wound they sent her from de island."

"But it was her home too," Susan interrupted.

Tantie placed her hand on Susan's head. "I know. But they believed she didn't leave de island and that she hid in de green jungle. Because whenever a man didn't come back from de jungle, or died a death they couldn't explain, they said that La Diablesse had lured him away. They said de devil gave her a cloven hoof to replace de right foot she had cut off. And some nights, especially rainy, stormy ones, they could hear a *Clop! Clop!* and they knew it was La Diablesse with her one good foot and her one cloven hoof stalking their village. And whenever she lured another man to his death, she rang a bell to take de place of her soundless scream.

"And that's La Diablesse's story," Tantie finished.

Just then the *Clang! Clang!* and the *Clop! Clop!* stopped

at the bedroom window. There was a strange noise and the window shook. I was sure La Diablesse was trying to come in. Avril trembled beside me.

"What La Diablesse want here?" he asked.

"Hello everybody, hello Tantie." It was Mama and Daddy in the doorway. They had come back from their fete.

"Duck down, Daddy!" I shouted. "La Diablesse trying to get in de house. She wants to lure a man to his death."

Daddy sat down fast fast. I guess he knew about La Diablesse too. But then Mama said, "All yuh know there's a cow outside? Wearing a bell and dragging a wooden stake, like she pull it up out of a field somewhere."

Me, Avril, Susan, Cedric, and Gerard all looked at each other and burst out laughing.

"Is only a cow, Tantie," said Avril, sounding relieved.

"Yes, dear," Tantie said. "It might only be a cow now, but next time it might be La Diablesse, so watch out. Don't let her lure you away anywhere."

I laughed but stopped quick quick when I saw Tantie's serious face. Avril looked like he was storing Tantie's advice for later use. I was thinking that history not so boring after all. It's just one big story about people.

Colin's Island

Dedicated to my grandmother,
LUCRETIA ALI-BUTTS
1907–1993

TANTIE'S STORIES ARE SO GOOD that I started writing them down. I wanted to make sure I remember the way she tell it. When I told her what I was doing, she just waved her hand and said, "By your mouth or on de paper, it don't matter as long as you pass them on. But a good storyteller stirs up de old words to make new soup."

One time, though, Tantie told me and my cousins a strange story about a mysterious island that rose out of the sea, and she said I shouldn't write it down.

It was the middle of August holidays, and the days were slow and sticky. It was rainy season, but no rain had fallen in two weeks. The rivers had dried into clumps of dirt and the frogs had left home. The grass was brown and sad. The street dogs and cats lay under the cars all day long hiding from the hot, waxy sun. Even the beach and tennis people closed their doors on August. Only us children were running around enjoying the days off from school like always.

We pitched marbles under the cherry tree. We held bike obstacle races around empty Coke bottles. We climbed the hills and mashed down trails with our dull cutlasses. We didn't care that everyone was complaining about the unusual weather.

Then one day, Tantie came by my house to visit with Mama. She was looking all fancied up, and she had a big grip with her.

"You going on a trip, Tantie?" I asked.

Tantie nodded.

"Where?" Avril asked.

Tantie put down her grip and took off her flower hat. "I going down south to Cedros, chile," said Tantie. "For a nice, quiet seaside holiday. All yuh ever heard of Cedros?"

Me and Avril looked at each other and at Susan, Cedric, and Gerard. I wasn't too sure where Cedros was, and I could tell they weren't either.

"No, Tantie," we muttered, kind of shameful.

"Good," Tantie said, with a big smile. "I hope them others don't know 'bout it either."

"Who is them others?" I asked.

"People with big, big eyes," said Tantie. She looked at each of us one by one, as if checking to see if any of us was one of them.

Tantie took off her dress shoes and put on her house slippers. Then she sat down on a brown hassock and called for my mama. "Sylvie," she said, "give me some coconut to grate while I tell these children about Cedros."

Mama handed Tantie a big bowl and some coconut chunks for grating. I thought Tantie would start telling a story right then, but instead she looked at me and said, "Don't write this one down, Amber. It could cause all kind of bacchanal."

"How?" I asked.

Tantie said, "When words written down neat neat and just so, is like people believe de story more. But this story I telling you could cause people to believe too much. Although this story true, we don't want people to think so."

Well, I wasn't sure what Tantie was talking about but I said okay. Then Tantie began her story.

"One rainy season, a long time ago, de rain forget to fall, just like this year. De rivers dried up and all de fish moved out to de sea. De sky was bright blue with no clouds. And de sun shine hot hot like a fire we couldn't put out. De fruits dried up on de tree branches like brown lumps. De whole island looked like it needed a cool, wet hug. And everybody wished for rain.

" 'If we only had some rain, we would never waste another drop,' de people said.

" 'If we only had some rain, we would be nice to each other all de time,' they said.

" 'If we only had some rain, we would be de happiest people in de world,' they said.

"But they didn't have any rain. So everyone quarreled about water.

" 'Why your car clean so?' a man asked his neighbor.

" 'My car ain't as clean as your hair,' said de neighbor. 'I en know about you but we en have extra water for no fancy hair washing.'

" 'My hair! What about them white, white shoes you wearing there? I know is not spit you spit to get them so clean. Must be water you using up to walk so la-de-da.'

"But one boy needed de rain more than anyone else. His granny was dying in Cedros, in a tiny house by de sea, down at de southern tip of de island. All Granny wanted before she said good-bye to de world was to see some flowers.

" 'But all de flowers are dead, Granny,' cried her grandson, Colin.

"Granny shook her head. 'There must be flowers somewhere. I have faith.' "

"Tantie," Avril interrupted. "You mean there wasn't a flower anywhere? In de whole island?"

Tantie nodded. "Yup," she said. "De place was dry like a monkey's eye at an alligator funeral.

"Anyway," Tantie continued, "Colin searched all over for flowers. He even went up to de big city, San Fernando, to de shops that sold flowers. But no one had any. Colin prayed for rain, so flowers would grow. But nothing happened. And each day he had to tell Granny, 'No flowers.'

"And she'd say, 'Yet.'

"One day, Colin sat on a large rock looking at de sun going down into de sea. Gold and orange sparkles flitted up from de water like mermaids' fingers reaching for de sky. Then darkness swooped down and lifted de sea-jewels, scattering them across de sky.

"Colin didn't have de energy to get up and go back to Granny's house without her flowers. 'O sea,' he said desperately, 'you are so wet and full of treasures, please give me a flower for my granny.'

"Colin's words floated over de sea. De waves hitting de rocks drowned him out. 'O sea,' Colin shouted, 'please share your treasures with me and I'll do anything you ask.'

"This time Colin's words did not float over de waves. They seemed to sink farther and farther down until they echoed with each wave hitting de rocks. De waves got blacker and wilder. Colin looked at them sadly, then trudged home.

"When Colin got to Granny's house, he thought he heard his name being whispered in de still trees. He looked around but everything was blackness. He peeped into Granny's room. And he stood stock still like de trees outside. Because all around Granny's bed were flowers. Red flowers, yellow ones, pink, purple, orange. And in de center was a big, beautiful sea-blue flower.

" 'Look, Colin,' Granny whispered. 'My flowers came.'

"Colin stared at de happy flowers in de room. Then there was a loud noise like de sky had cracked open. And at last come de sound of rain. Heavy, wet, wonderful raindrops. Colin and Granny looked in each other's eyes and knew their prayers were answered. Colin went to bed with de sound of rain like a hand patting his head."

"Where de flowers come from, Tantie?" Susan asked, her eyes big and round.

Tantie shrugged. "Some things we don't wonder about too much because we go never find de answer."

"But, Tantie, you think Colin knew where de flowers came from?" I asked.

"No," said Tantie, "but I en finish de story yet.

"De next morning, Colin woke early. De rain hadn't stopped. De drops tapped on his window, calling to him.

"Colin got up and opened de window. There sitting smack dab in de middle of de sea, straight out from de beach in front of Granny's home, was a small, glistening, black island.

"Colin squeezed his eyes shut tightly and opened them again. De island was still there, sparkling in de rain.

" 'Oh my gosh,' said Colin. He pulled on his swim trunks and ran outside to de beach. He didn't even think about being scared. He just dove between de waves and swam straight for de island.

"As he pulled himself up onto de island, Colin understood why it was black and shining in de rain. Instead of dirt or sand, de island was covered in thick, black oil. Streams of oil flowed across it into black pools.

"Colin looked around slowly. He swished his hand through de oil. Then he tore a strip of cloth from his shorts and found a stick to tie it to. Colin planted his homemade flag in de thickest clump of oil he could find. De flag waved in de first cool breeze of de season. 'Colin's Island,' he said softly.

"De rain fell and fell on Colin and on de island. Colin could see de people on de mainland busy collecting rainwater in buckets and barrels. Nobody seemed to notice de island. That was fine with Colin.

"He sat and thought. De sea must have answered my wish

for treasure. It helped bring de flowers and de rain, and now this island. But what does it want from me?

"Colin looked down at his oil-covered legs and feet. He looked at de sea sitting quiet and blue except for de *plip plop* of raindrops striking de surface. He looked at de island—small, perfect, and wrapped in black glory.

"All day and night, Colin sat on his island feeling de wonderful rain fall on his head and shoulders. He felt he must wait for something, but he didn't know what. Then as de sky cleared, Colin's thoughts played out like a magical painting across de sky. And he saw all that would soon happen. People would come to his island. They would fight over de lovely dark oil. Strangers from other lands would come to gather up his oil and plunge huge machines into his quiet, blue sea to find more oil. De fish would die and lie rotting on de beach. The turtles would drown in de choked waters. He would not be able to swim at Cedros anymore. Or walk on de beach because his feet would stick to de tar-covered sand.

"Colin began to cry. His tears mixed with de oil. 'Go away,' he cried to his tiny island. 'Go away.'

"Then Colin dove into de sea and swam back to Granny's house. He fell asleep as de sun began to rise.

"When he woke up, de sun was high in de sky, daring de islanders to wish for more rain. Colin looked out his window. His island was gone! There was no shiny black anything, only blue, blue water all around.

" 'It's gone,' he cried. 'Granny, it's gone.'

"But Granny shook her head. 'What you talking 'bout, boy?'

" 'De island that rose out de sea yesterday—it's gone,' said Colin, happily.

" 'Colin, stop that nonsense,' said Granny. 'I been looking out this window all day yesterday at de rain. Ain't no island rise out de sea here.'

"Colin heard de same thing all day. It was as if he had dreamed de island. De villagers laughed at him when he mentioned it.

" 'You been drinking too much rainwater, boy,' they said.

" 'No, no, his throat was so parched, it affect his brain,' they said.

" 'So, what your little island like, Colin? You go be prime minister and all?' They laughed at him.

"But Colin didn't say anything. He went back to Granny's house and sat on his bed. He wondered if he was going crazy. De island had been so real to him.

"Then Colin saw it. Lying on de floor in a corner was de pair of swim trunks from yesterday. It was covered in black oil. Colin smiled. And he went to bury de swim trunks deep in de backyard. He would never tell a soul about his oil discovery. Colin's mysterious island would be his own forever.

"And after his granny died, surrounded by rainbows of beautiful flowers, Colin spent many years walking on de clean Cedros sand and swimming in de clear blue sea."

Tantie handed us each a small piece of coconut to chew

on. She dusted off some coconut from her lap. The story was finished. But neither me, nor Avril, Cedric, Susan, nor Gerard moved. I was thinking about the story.

Finally, I said, "Tantie, is a lot of questions I have about that story. Did Colin figure out what de sea wanted from him?"

"Well, Amber," said Tantie. "You could decide that for yourself. Some stories are like that. It go be different for each person. That's another reason why we don't write them down. Because then it's only one way."

Avril spoke up. "I think de sea was giving Colin a present in de small oil island. I mean, Colin did ask for some treasure. But Colin didn't want de sea's gift, right, Tantie?"

"What do you think?" Tantie asked.

Avril sucked on his coconut and was quiet. Tantie looked at me.

"I think Colin felt he had enough gifts from de sea already," I said. "De fish and de clean beach and de clear blue water for him to swim in. He didn't need an oil island too."

"Yeah, but Colin could have been rich," said Cedric.

"Depends on how you measure your riches," said Tantie. Cedric looked at her, puzzled.

"Tantie," I said, "I think de sea wasn't expecting anything back from Colin. It was just giving him gifts. And letting him choose which gifts he wanted to keep forever."

Tantie didn't answer, but I could see a look in her eye that was like a smile. Then she waved her hands at us. "All yuh remember de story, but no writing it down, Amber."

A long time after Tantie told this story, a big announce-

ment came over the Trinidad television. Oil had been dis-
covered off Cedros Point. A big foreign oil company was
coming to set up oil rigs and do some drilling. The whole
island was buzzing with the talk of oil and riches.

Tantie came over that night, her head hanging low and
her mouth set grim grim.

"Amber," she said, "they done opened their big, big eyes
and found Colin's island. We go take one gift from de sea
and mash up all de rest, just like Colin saw would happen.
You might as well write down that story now. We reach de
ending."

So I wrote it down. But Tantie's right. Sometimes it best
not to write a story down neat neat and just so. Because then
the ending can't change, and people might believe it too
much.

Tantie's Callaloo Fete

*E*VERY YEAR, Tantie throws a big callaloo fete to celebrate the origin of Trinidad culture. People start talking about Tantie's callaloo party long before she even buys the crabs and picks the dasheen to make the callaloo. This year was no different.

"All yuh going to Tantie's callaloo fete? I hear de crabs sweet for so," said Punchie, who sells newspapers on the corner near my house.

"I en miss one of Tantie's callaloo parties yet—you mad or what?" said Florentine, the tall woman who sells channa and peanuts next to Punchie.

"You going this year, Amber?" they both asked me.

"Yup." I nodded my head and tried not to smile too big. But they smiled bigger than ever for me because they knew I'd been waiting a long time to go to one of Tantie's callaloo fetes.

The fete was for grown-ups, because it was an all-night

party. This was the first year that me and Avril could go, and we couldn't wait.

We had heard plenty about the singing, dancing, and eating at the callaloo fete. At the stroke of midnight, Tantie would scrape down to the bun bun of the callaloo pot and dish out the last bit onto plates and bowls. But she would leave in the crab claws. Then everybody would pitch a treasure into the pot, something they had brought to the party for the treasure pot. It could be anything, as long as it had some meaning to the owner. One by one the callaloo eaters would go up to the big iron pot with eyes closed and reach in for a treasure. Of course, the treasure would have some green callaloo on it, but nobody minded. Some people pulled out a crab claw as their treasure. These were the best because it meant good luck for the whole year.

At home, Mama and Daddy talked about Tantie's callaloo party too. Me and Avril were sitting on the front porch, and heard them.

"Honey, where Tantie getting de crabs this year?" asked Mama.

"I en know," said Daddy. "I suppose she go get them from de crab man like always."

"No," Mama said. "De crab man moved to de States with his sister."

"Well, I hope he show somebody where he got those delicious crabs from, cause they were de best."

"That's what I worried about," said Mama. "How Tantie go make her callaloo this year if de crab man gone?"

When me and Avril heard this, we got worried. Suppose

Tantie had to cancel the fete this year because of the crab man!

"Let's ride our bikes over there tomorrow," said Avril. "See if we can help."

"Okay," I agreed.

The next day, me and Avril got up extra early. We met at Four Roads corner and started riding fast fast to Tantie's house before the morning traffic began honking and beeping. The air swished by fresh and cool, since the sun wasn't high enough yet to dry last night's raindrops.

Tantie's windows and doors were thrown wide open already. A lonely red rocker sat quietly on the porch. As we parked our bikes, Tantie came out the side door. She wore an apron over her yellow cooking dress.

She didn't say hello. She just handed us each a banana and smiled.

"Tantie," Avril started, as he peeled his banana, "you still having your callaloo fete this year?"

"Course, chile, nothing go stop de callaloo fete. There's been one every year since before I was born." Tantie shook out her apron and white flour dust floated to the ground.

"But Mama said your crab man gone to de States," I said. "How you go make callaloo without crabs?"

"And what about de crab claws treasure?" asked Avril. "De pot have to have crab claws, right?"

Tantie put up a hand to hush us. She climbed the front steps to the porch and sat down in her red rocker, which creaked in greeting.

"Oh, to rest my weary bones," she said softly. "Now, all

yuh two sit up here cause I got something very important to tell yuh."

Me and Avril hurriedly put the kickstands down on our bikes and sat down by Tantie's feet.

"Is it a story?" asked Avril.

Tantie nodded and said, "I go tell all yuh about de first callaloo fete and how it happened. Once you know that, you will see why nothing could stop de party.

"Years and years ago, Trinidad was an island with a new ship in de harbor every week. Plenty people were coming here from all over de world. We had de Spanish, and French, and British; then Africans, Chinese, and East Indians; and Syrians, Portuguese, and then some from Venezuela.

"Everybody had their own language and their own clothes and songs and food. We were all different."

Me and Avril looked at each other. I was wondering what this had to do with a callaloo party. Tantie must have seen the look because she cleared her throat and boomed, "This was before anyone had even heard of callaloo.

"But de one thing everybody had that was de same was that they were trying to make Trinidad their home. They built houses and planted fields and fished in de sea, whether they were Chinese or African or French or Indian.

"One rainy season, a big tropical storm swept through the Caribbean. Usually Trinidad doesn't have a problem with these storms because it not in de eye path. But this storm was so big and strong that it raged through like a beast trampling over de island and kicking it into de sky.

"When de island landed back on de sea and de beast moved

on, everything was a mess. Crops were drowned, houses flattened, and many people dead. De survivors shook their heads sadly and started building back their homes right away. But their crops were going to take some time. Most of de people didn't have any food.

"Everyone looked around and wondered what to do. Then a smart woman found her big cooking pot and set it up in de middle of town. And she started to cook a big pot of soup. She invited everyone—all de Chinese, and de Africans, and de French, and de Indians—to come and add something to de pot of soup. And everyone did.

"De Africans came with a big, green leafy plant called callaloo bush. They tore it into strips and put it in de pot. The soup turned a dark-green color and was thick with callaloo bush. Then de Chinese came with green seedpods called okra and added them to de soup. Then de Indians came with a piece of yellow pumpkin and dropped it into de pot. De Spanish came with a bowl of coconut milk and poured it into de soup. De French came with garlic, onions, thyme, and chives they found that had survived de storm. And last of all, de children from all de different groups brought bushels of blue crabs that they caught on de beach after de storm. De children washed out de crabs and added them to de pot of soup. Then de smart woman stirred and stirred de big pot of soup."

"Tantie, who was this woman? Which of de groups she was from?" I asked.

Tantie shook her head. "It don't matter one bit which group she was from.

"When de soup was ready, de smart woman called it callaloo. She dished out bowl after bowl of de delicious, thick, green soup and everyone sat down to eat. When they finished, they put de crab claws back into de pot to be saved for another callaloo soup. From then on de different people became friends and shared their music and stories and food with one another. And they each learned to make callaloo, which became Trinidad's national dish.

"De children who caught de crabs grew up and married each other, not caring who came from which group. And their children, who were half-Chinese, half-African, or half-Indian, half-French, were called callaloo children. And to this day, most Trinidadians are callaloo children because everyone stayed friends and kept marrying from all de different groups."

Tantie looked from me to Avril. "So, all yuh see why we must keep de callaloo fete going?"

Avril nodded. "To feed everybody," he said.

"Not just that," I said, poking Avril in his belly. "Is to remember how everybody got to be friends in de first place."

"Both of all yuh are right," said Tantie. "So I expect both of you to help me with de callaloo soup this year."

"Can we go to de beach and catch de crabs de way de children did for de first callaloo soup?" Avril asked.

Tantie smiled. "Well, I do need those crab claws. And you could ask Gerard and Susan and Cedric to help you. Is plenty crabs I need for de callaloo."

Then I thought of something. "Tantie," I said, "if me and Avril get our cousins to help us catch de crabs, how come they can't come to de callaloo party too? I think de children added de best part to de first callaloo soup, so how come children can't come to de fete till we grown up?"

After I said all that I sat down quiet quiet and held my breath. I was scared of what Tantie might say. She don't tolerate no back talk from nobody, and I sounded like I was talking back.

After a few minutes, Tantie reached over and hugged me hard. I was surprised.

She looked me right in the eye and said, "I so glad I have you, Amber. You see what I don't see and you tell what you must." Then she smiled. "From now on we go invite everybody to come to de callaloo fete, old and young, because you right, Amber. De children added de best thing of all."

Me and Avril jumped up and cheered. We hurried home on our bikes. We had plenty crabs to catch for de party and we had to get started right away.

The next week, everyone went to Tantie's callaloo party—me, Avril, Cedric, Susan, Gerard, and all the baby cousins too. We ate bowl after bowl of callaloo, and when the sun went down, we joined in the calypso singing.

As it got later, Tantie tucked the baby cousins into her big iron bed. By midnight, even Susan, Cedric, and Gerard had gone to sleep in Tantie's bedroom. But not me and Avril. We were patiently waiting for Tantie to scrape the bottom of the callaloo pot.

When she did, and the treasures were put in, Avril pulled out a small jar of guava jam. I closed my eyes and reached in next. I pulled out a crab claw! The first one for the night!

Everyone cheered. I smiled at Tantie because I knew my good luck for the upcoming year would include her.

As the night turned into morning, people began to hug and kiss each other good-bye. Everyone was saying how this was the best callaloo fete ever. Although me and Avril had never been to any other, we soundly agreed.

The Obeah Woman's
Birthday Present

Since me and Avril were old enough now for grown-up fetes, we couldn't imagine going to a little kid's birthday party anymore. Not even when Gerard was turning ten years old and his mama, Auntie Mary, was planning a big party for him.

"You going?" Avril asked, as he caught a mango I threw down from the top of the mango tree. We were going to make mango chow.

"You mad or what? De party is only for little children."

"Yeah," said Avril. "They probably go be playing Pop de Balloon or Musical Chairs like always."

"Catch!" I shouted and threw another half-ripe mango at him. Then I began to climb back down the tree.

"They probably go wear silly birthday hats too," I said.

"Yeah, we too old for all that," said Avril.

But neither me nor Avril had reckoned with Tantie. She

was standing at the back door of my house and had heard the whole thing.

"So, all yuh bodies grow an inch, and yuh hearts shrink a mile?" Tantie snapped, as we carried the mangoes inside.

"Whatcha mean, Tantie?" Avril asked.

But I already had a feeling what Tantie was talking about.

"All yuh can't go to your cousin's party because yuh too big, eh? Well, let me tell you something. Selfish monkeys lose their hearts, but foolish monkeys can find theirs back."

I saw Avril's face looking even more puzzled.

"What that mean, Tantie?" he asked.

I nudged him to hush up. "It mean we going to Gerard's party, Avril," I said. And I gave Tantie a quick smile.

"So we going?" he asked.

"Yes," I answered. "But I not doing any of those baby things."

"Maybe you could tell a story to the kids," said Avril.

I shrugged my shoulders. "I en know if I have one to tell," I muttered. "It hard hard to come up with a story just so. I en know how Tantie does it. Tantie says I'll start to feel the right story in my bones, and the words will just flow out. But it hasn't happened to me yet."

Well, Gerard's birthday came on a bright, sunny day two weeks after Christmas. It was the kind of day when the whole family would pack up the car with a big pot of pelau and a cooler full of banana sweet drinks and head for Maracas Beach. But instead of going to the beach to play cricket on the sand and jump up in the waves, me and Avril got dressed up for Gerard's party. I was sorry we had decided to go after all. And so was Avril.

"You shouldn't have said we were going," he muttered.

"It too hot for these frilly clothes," I grumbled.

"Only going to be a bunch of kids there," he said.

"And baby games," I agreed.

When we got to the party, the first person I saw was Tantie. She was helping Auntie Mary put the snacks on the table in the front yard. I gave a quick curtsey to Tantie and kissed her cheek. But she was too busy to talk. She waved her hand and kept on fixing the table.

Me and Avril followed Auntie Mary inside the big house. The living room was covered in balloons and colorful drawings.

"De children had their drawing contest already," said Auntie Mary. "They out in de backyard now playing."

Me and Avril walked on to the backyard where a full-swing party was happening. Gerard was wearing a big, blue Happy Birthday hat and showing off a paper trophy. When he saw us, he came running over.

"Look what I win!" he boasted, swinging his trophy high in the air. "I draw de best picture out of everybody. And you see all my friends from school," he shouted, pointing to the mass of children running around and throwing balls.

Avril ducked as a ball sailed by and almost knocked off his head. Gerard gave a big laugh and ran off.

"Kids," grumbled Avril. "I en know about you, but I going back in to help Tantie and Auntie Mary."

As we turned to go inside, I saw an old woman come up to the back gate.

"Happy Birthday, boy! Where's de happy birthday boy?" she called.

"Hey, Avril, wait," I said. "That not de whistling woman from up de street?"

The woman was very wrinkly. She wore a beautiful red party dress and black sandals with shiny stones on the front. And she was carrying a small, wrapped present. Avril and I watched as she handed it to Gerard.

"I ain't never seen her in anything but a brown dress before," said Avril. "And she usually sitting on her front porch."

"Well, it look like she coming to this party," I said quietly.

Just as soon as I said that, Gerard threw the woman's gift across the fence and slammed the gate shut so she couldn't come in.

"You not invited," he shouted. All the children began to gather around. "Go away, wrinkly woman," said Gerard in a louder voice. And the children laughed.

Me and Avril watched with our mouths open. We had never seen Gerard act so rudely before.

"He showing off," said Avril with disgust. I had to agree.

We could hear the old woman whistling as she trudged up the street. Just then Tantie came out of the house. From the look on her face, I could tell she had seen what had happened. Gerard go get it now, I thought. But Tantie didn't say a word about it. Instead, she clapped her hands. "Cake and ice cream on de front porch for all yuh. Come on, birth-day boy."

We followed Gerard inside. I looked back over my shoulder as the old woman's whistle drifted away.

The birthday table was set up like a feast, with two cakes, currant rolls, and coconut buns. There were also bowls of plums and pommeracs and a plate of channa pies. And at one end of the table was a huge ice-cream freezer filled with barbadine ice cream. Me and Avril looked at each other with big smiles. I knew he was thinking the same thing I was— that this party not so bad after all.

Avril didn't wait for the birthday boy to get his plate first. He filled up a plate fast fast and was sitting on a bench eating before any of us. Tantie only chuckled at him.

I got a plate and sat next to Avril. But I couldn't eat. I was wondering why Tantie didn't say anything to Gerard about the whistling woman. She usually get real strict if any of us act rude or give back talk.

After everyone had finished eating, Gerard asked Tantie for a story. Tantie always tells a story at our birthday parties before we cut the cake. But this time, Tantie shook her head no.

"I don't have any today, chile. All my stories dry up. But maybe your cousin Amber got one for you." And Tantie give me one good, hard look so that I feel my hands shaking.

It was like she was talking to me in my head. I could almost hear her voice even though she wasn't saying anything aloud.

Then all at once I felt the story in my bones. The words were ready to flow right out. I jumped up and clapped my hands like I had seen Tantie do a hundred times when she wanted to get our attention.

"All yuh want to hear a story?" I asked loudly. "This is a special story for a birthday boy." I moved over and made a place for Gerard on my right as all his friends gathered around. Then I started to tell my story.

"Not long ago, an old woman lived alone in a big empty house. She didn't have any friends. Everyone was scared of her because she was an obeah woman. De only people who visited this obeah woman were those that wanted secret potions to put curses on their enemies. De obeah woman put all kinds of strange things in her secret potions like goat livers and frog gizzards and pieces of de enemy's body, like their fingernails or eyelashes."

"Their eyelashes!" said Gerard. "Yuck!"

"Yeah, yuck!" shouted the little kids.

I could hear Avril snickering softly behind me. I ignored him and went on.

"Eyelashes were good if de obeah woman couldn't get their eyes. Eyes made even stronger potions." The little kids shivered and moved closer together.

"Anyway, this obeah woman was lonely from not having any friends. So, she moved to another big, empty house, and she made sure not to tell anybody that she was an obeah woman. She walked up and down de street whistling songs to let people know how friendly she was. And she sat on her front porch and waved at people as they walked by. But no one made friends with her. So she decided to be more bold. When she heard that a child on de street was having a birthday party, she decided that she would go and take a present. She looked around her house for de right thing.

" 'I bound to have something here for a boy,' she muttered, as she looked under her books, and in between her shoes, and on top of her stove. But she didn't have anything suited for a boy. So, de obeah woman sat and thought. Until she came up with de perfect present.

"She took out her huge potion-mixing bowl, which she had brought with her to de new house in case of emergencies. And she began pouring wonderful things into it. Bright red hibiscus flowers, and two ripe mangoes. A pretty snakeskin that glistened with many colors when de sun hit it. She also put in a beautiful song and a colorful kite."

Then Gerard interrupted me. "But, Amber, how can de obeah woman put a song in de bowl?"

"De obeah woman sang de song right into de bowl and swirled it around and around until it mixed right in with de flowers and de mangoes," I answered.

"When everything was mixed just right, de obeah woman poured it all into a glass jar and pushed a cork in. Then she wrapped de jar in shiny yellow paper and got dressed for de birthday party."

"What was de secret potion for?" Susan asked.

"You'll find out," I said.

Then I felt a tug on my arm. I looked down at Gerard.

"What did de obeah woman wear to de party?" he asked in a whisper.

"Oh, she wore de only dress she had—a simple brown thing with her old brown shoes."

"Oh," he sighed.

"But it was a magic dress," I continued, "because whoever looked at it saw a beautiful red party dress instead of de old brown one." I didn't look back at Gerard, but I could hear him suck in his breath.

"Anyway, de obeah woman took her present and walked down de street to de boy's house. There was a big, happy birthday party going on. She heard de loud music and de screams of excitement from de children playing in de yard.

"Finally, I go make some friends, she thought. She couldn't wait to go inside and play and color pictures and eat cake and ice cream. At least that's what she thought she would do at de party. She wasn't sure, because she had never been to a birthday party before. When she got to de gate of de house, she called out to de birthday child.

" 'Happy Birthday, boy!' she said. She smiled at de little boy.

"But he didn't see her smile. 'Go away,' he shouted.

"She tried to give him her present. But he pitched it far over de fence and laughed.

"Well, that was his big mistake. He could have turned de old woman away, and it would have been okay. But when he threw her present away, it sailed through de air and landed with a big thump and broke. And de magic potion that was supposed to be locked up forever in de jar spilled all over de ground."

"What was de magic potion for?" whispered Gerard.

"It was to keep de boy young forever. And when it spilled, de old woman looked at it sadly and walked away, whistling all de way home."

"Why?" asked Gerard.

"Because de obeah woman knew she couldn't stop what would happen to de boy. Instead of staying young forever, now he would grow old fast."

"How fast?" asked Gerard in a scared voice.

"Very fast," I answered. "So fast that every day when he got up and looked in de mirror, he wouldn't recognize himself. His birthdays would come faster and faster, until almost every day was his birthday, or so it would seem to him. And in de mirror he would see mean wrinkles growing all over his face."

"But why she couldn't stop de magic potion from doing this to him if she made it herself?" Gerard asked frantically.

"Well, only de boy could stop it. She had no control once he threw her gift away. And only de boy knew what to do. No one else knew and no one could help him."

"Well, what happened to de obeah woman?" asked Avril.

"De obeah woman went back to sit on her porch."

All of a sudden, Gerard jumped up, grabbed a coconut bun from the table, and ran inside the house. We heard the backyard gate swing open and then slam shut. And that's when Tantie started clapping. But this time she wasn't clapping to get attention. She was clapping for my story and smiling a big smile.

The next thing we knew, Gerard was walking through the house leading the wrinkly woman by one hand. He pulled her through the front door and onto the porch. In her other hand was a coconut bun. And she was smiling.

On the way home from the party, Avril turned to me and said, "So, is a good thing we went to that party, eh?"

I nodded. It was a good thing for me because for the first time I felt what it was like to be a storyteller.

"Amber, she not really an obeah woman, is she?" Avril asked.

"Of course she is, Avril. You didn't see when she spilled some juice on her dress that de red disappeared in that spot and it was brown underneath?"

Avril gave me such a frightened look that I busted out laughing and couldn't stop all the way home.

Afterword

Trinidad's folklore embraces a spectrum of mythical characters from all around the world. That's because the people of Trinidad come from many countries: Africa, India, France, England, China, Syria, Spain, and Venezuela. When the stories from these different peoples meshed up together, they formed a unique folklore that was all and only Trinidadian in form and language and figure. It includes creatures like the jumbies, who are Trinidad's bogeymen. They are the spirits of the dead who play pranks on the unsuspecting. And La Diablesse (la ja BLESS), who is of predominantly African origin, with both French and Spanish influences.

La Diablesse is one of Trinidad's favorite characters. She is most often depicted as having a distorted, hideous face, which she covers with a straw hat. She appears to men as a beautiful creature at parties. She loves to dance, and she will dance an unsuspecting man right away into the forest where he will either die by falling off a cliff or be found later in a state of shock. La Diablesse has one foot, the left, and one cloven hoof where her right foot should be. La Diablesse does not have a shadow, and she glides over the ground as if walking on the air.

Trinidad's folklore creatures also include the duennes (DWENZ). The duennes are playful "Little People" who wear broad-brimmed straw hats over their pigtails. They are mischievous elves, believed to be the spirits of babies who died before they could be christened. The duennes often cluster in groups near riverbanks and call out to other unchristened children to lure them away into the forest.

Obeah men and women are Trinidad's black-magic people. Some obeahs are medicine people who help heal and cure diseases or other maladies, from a swollen toe to a cutlass slash. Some will concoct potions to cast spells on others for a price. Obeahs in Trinidad villages may function as psychiatrists or psychics. They will listen to a person's troubles and give advice, and usually some sort of potion or herbs as well. An obeah might foresee your troubles and predict your future. The obeah will often come to the home of the person who needs a curse or a helpful potion and do a dance-chant around the backyard, shaking a bag of bones. All obeahs are feared and respected for their power and magic.

Along with their love for a good story, Trinidadians, as a nation, enjoy a year-round, festive atmosphere of parties, celebrations, and cultural and religious fetes that include their favorite pastime: eating delicious foods.

The foods mentioned in these stories may be found at any

local gathering of two or more people, as well as more traditional events. Pelau is a beach-party natural because everything goes into one big pot: browned-down rice, chicken or beef, pumpkin, and pigeon peas. Add lots of hot pepper and it's ready. Mauby is a true thirst-quencher made from boiling and purifying mauby bark, which comes from a tree. Channa is another name for chick peas, which are soaked in salt water and then fried in oil with seasonings and pepper. They look like and are eaten like salted nuts. Pommerac and barbadine are tropical fruits. Pommerac is often made into a jam, and barbadine makes wonderful ice cream and creamy drinks. Mango chow is for the very brave because it's so spicy. It is made from half-ripe mangoes, still green and firm. The mangoes are sliced into a bowl of vinegar, salt, and hot pepper. After the fruit has soaked up the spiciness for a while, it's ready to be eaten.

LYNN JOSEPH grew up listening to stories like those in this book. She was born on the island of Trinidad, in the West Indies, and later moved with her family to Baltimore, Maryland. She received a bachelor's degree from the University of Colorado and a law degree from Fordham University School of Law. Ms. Joseph is now an attorney in New York City, where she lives with her husband, Ed, and their son, Jared. Her previous books for Clarion are *A Wave in Her Pocket: Stories from Trinidad* and *An Island Christmas*.

DONNA PERRONE, a native New Yorker, enjoyed drawing with chalks as a child. She studied painting at the School of Visual Arts, received a bachelor's degree, then spent a year reacquainting herself with chalk pastels, the medium she still prefers. Ms. Perrone developed an interest in Caribbean art while teaching children in a special program at SVA, and she plans to combine teaching with her illustration work. *The Mermaid's Twin Sister* is her first book.